artdecade monthly

2019 collection

artdecade monthly 2019 collection

selected works
from the galleries of
artdecademonthly.com

published and distributed by
furplanet.com

adults only

COACH

ZZZ...

HNNG!

...

BOY...

HOW MANY TIMES HAVE I TOLD YOU TO PUT DOWN A DAMN TOWEL?

HEH HEH...

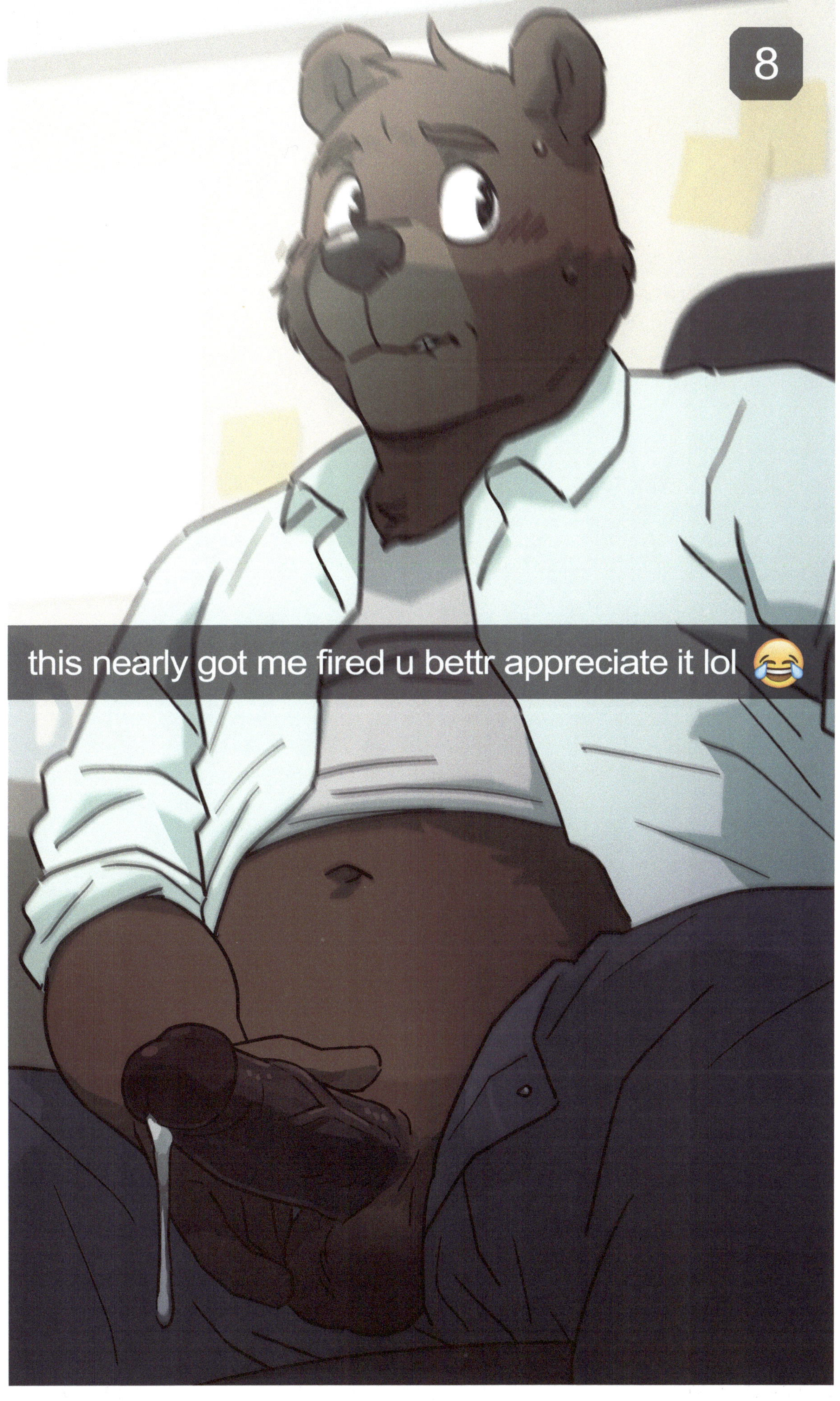
8
this nearly got me fired u bettr appreciate it lol 😂

TRICK or TREAT
FROM WILLY&PALS
2019
HAPPY HALLOWEEN!

TRICK or TREAT
FROM WILLY&PALS
2019
HAPPY HALLOWEEN!
TRICK or TREAT
FROM WILLY&PALS
2019
HAPPY HALLOWEEN!

TRICK or TREAT
FROM WILLY&PALS
2019
HAPPY HALLOWEEN!
TRICK or TREAT
FROM WILLY&PALS
2019
HAPPY HALLOWEEN!

7
Lookin' good, pops!

YOU DON'T MIND IF I HELP MYSELF?

DAS KAPITAL

4
Told ya.

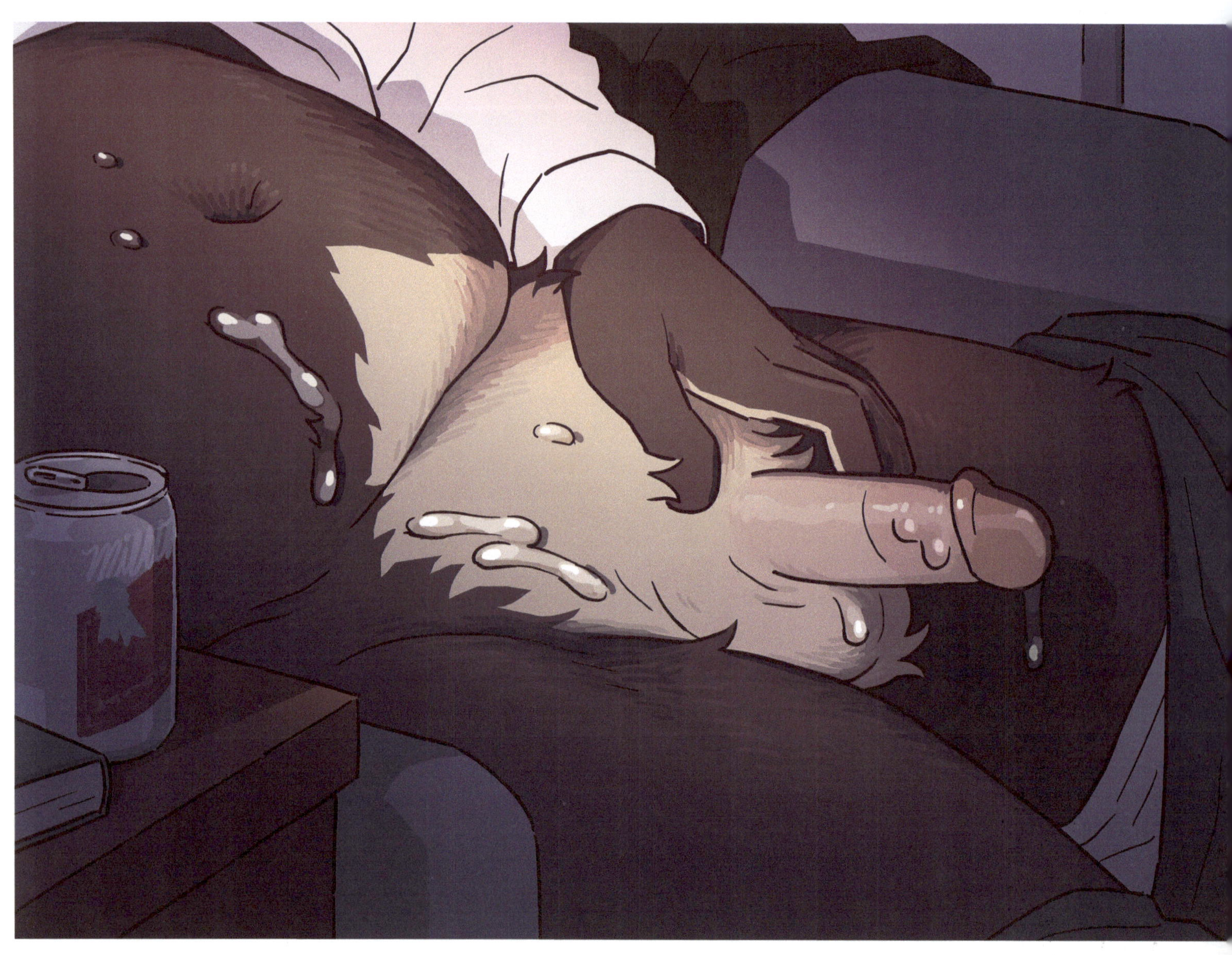

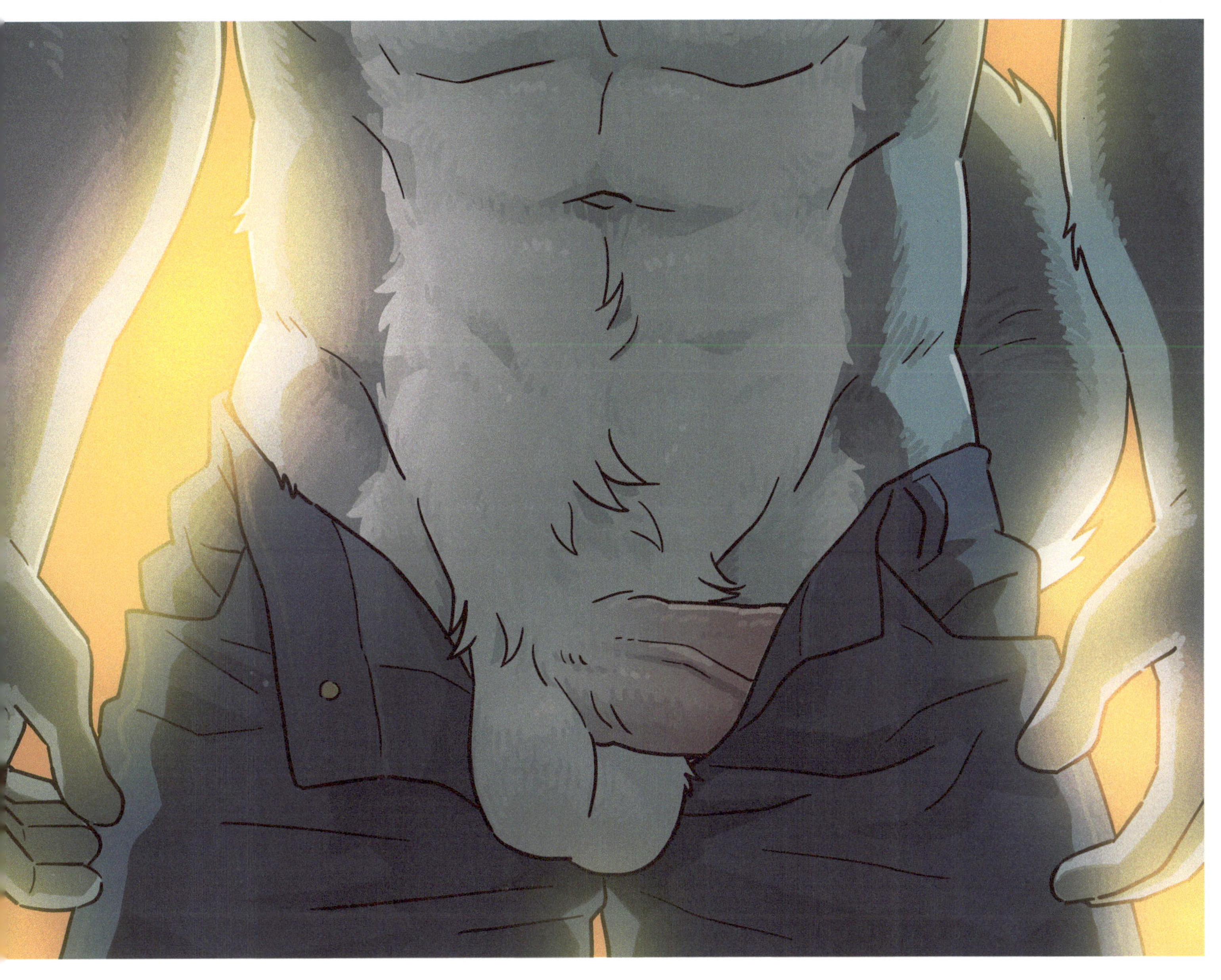

artdecademonthly.com

artdecademonthly.com

artdecademonthly.com

artdecademonthly.com

artdecademonthly.com

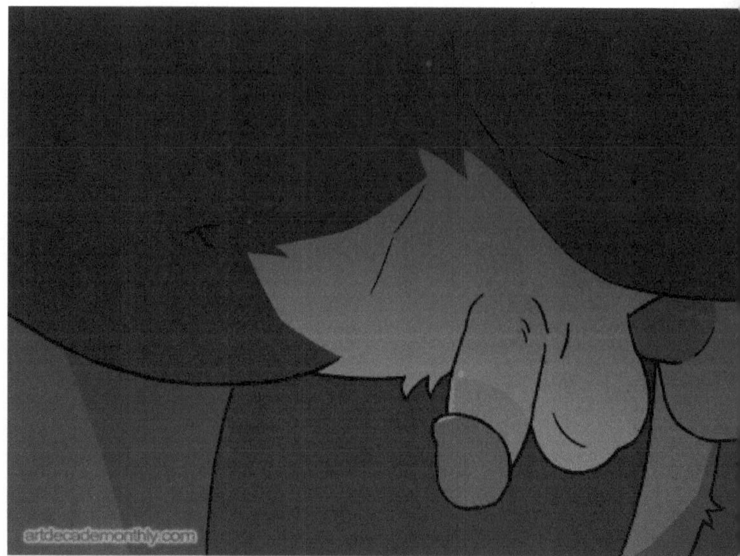
artdecademonthly.com

THE TIMES

THE TIMES

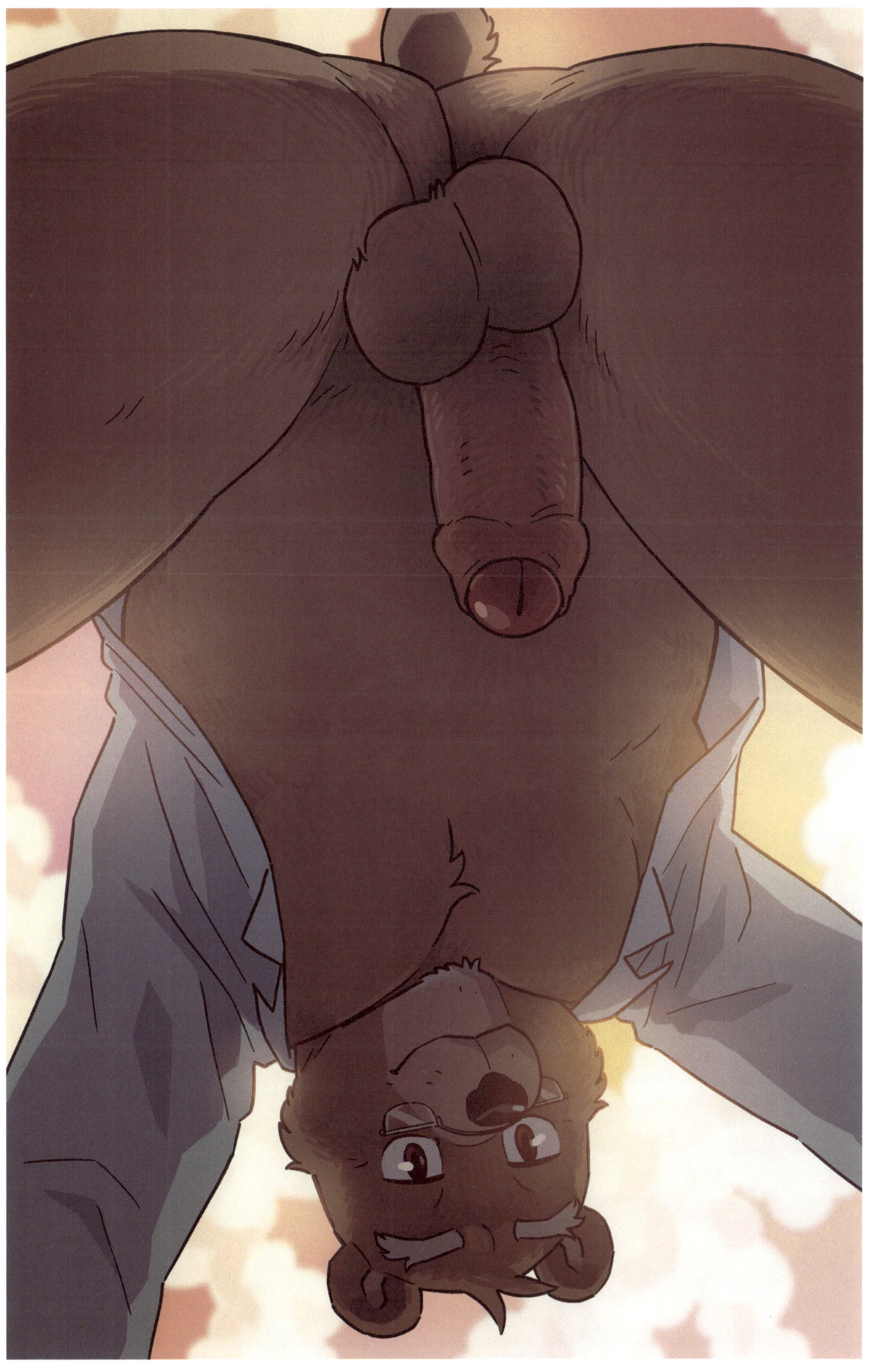

www.ingramcontent.com/pod-product-compliance
Lightning Source LLC
LaVergne TN
LVHW070509120826
845147LV00031BA/276
9781614506270